SPOOKTACULAR JOKE BOOK

Written by Jim Bernstein and Scott Peterson

Based on the series created by Dan Povenmire & Jeff "Swampy" Marsh

DISNEY PRESS

New York

Copyright © 2012 Disney Enterprises, Inc.
All rights reserved. Published by Disney Press, an imprint of
Disney Book Group. No part of this book may be reproduced or
transmitted in any form or by any means, electronic or mechanical,
including photocopying, recording, or by any information storage
and retrieval system, without written permission from the
publisher. For information address Disney Press, 114 Fifth Avenue,
New York, New York 10011-5690.

Printed in the United States of America

First Edition

1 3 5 7 9 10 8 6 4 2

J689-1817-1-10335
Library of Congress Control Number: 2012933314
ISBN 978-1-4231-5372-6

For more Disney Press fun, visit www.disneybooks.com
Visit DisneyChannel.com

If you purchased this book without a cover, you should be aware
that this book is stolen property. It was reported as "unsold
and destroyed" to the publisher, and neither the author nor the
publisher has received any payment for this "stripped" book.

It was a dark and spooky night in Phineas and Ferb's backyard. The kids sat around a blazing campfire.

"Ferb, I know what we're gonna do tonight," Phineas said. "Let's tell scary stories and jokes!"

"Cool!" Isabella exclaimed.

"*Bo*-ring," Candace complained. "Mom said I had to keep an eye on you dweebs, but she didn't say I had to listen to dumb, little kiddie stories all night!"

"I don't know, Candace," Phineas said with a smile. "These tales can get *pretty* spooky. . . ."

"Like this story," Phineas said. "I like to call this one 'The Creature!' There once was a young inventor. He was a true genius but also very lazy, too lazy to even make his bed. So he decided to build a creature to do it for him."

"Would it not have been easier just to make his own bed?" Baljeet wondered.

"Shhh," Isabella said. "Let him finish!"

Phineas continued. "The boy spent many days and nights in his laboratory, doing indescribable things with lightning, chicken parts, and his dad's corduroy pants to create a strange and unearthly creature. He became obsessed. He would complete his creation if it was the last thing he did!"

"This is going to end badly," said Buford. "They *always* end badly!"

Phineas took a deep breath. "Then, late one night . . . in the glow of the full moon . . . the creature . . . finally . . . moved! The boy laughed maniacally. 'Alive! He's alive!'

"The monster slowly rose up and faced the boy, towering over him. The boy ordered the creature to make his bed.

"The creature glared at him and growled: 'MAKE IT YOURSELF, LAZY!'"

"That's *it*?" Candace asked. "Sounds like the storyteller was the lazy one to me!"

"Well, I thought it was great," said Isabella. "Speaking of mad scientists, I heard some funny **MAD SCIENTIST JOKES** at my Fireside Girls meeting last week. Want to hear some?"

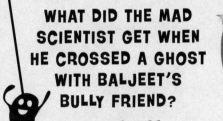

WHAT DID THE MAD SCIENTIST GET WHEN HE CROSSED A GHOST WITH BALJEET'S BULLY FRIEND?

Boo-ford!

WHAT DID THE MAD DOCTOR SAY TO HIS PATIENT, THE INVISIBLE MAN?

I don't see anything wrong with you!

"I've got some jokes about extraterrestrials," Baljeet offered.

"We've got enough terrestrials as it is," Buford snapped. "We don't need any extras." Then he paused. "Uh, what's a *terrestrial*?" he asked.

Baljeet sighed. "Extraterrestrials are visitors from outer space!"

"Ohhhhhh," Buford said. "**ALIEN JOKES!** Why didn't you say so?"

WHY DO MARTIANS ALWAYS HAVE SUCH NICE-LOOKING PLANTS?

They have green thumbs!

HOW MANY ALIENS DOES IT TAKE TO SCREW IN SEVEN LIGHTBULBS?

One—as long as he has seven arms!

WHAT DOES MEAP USE TO CLEAN THE SPACE BETWEEN THE PLANETS?

A vacuum cleaner!

"I've got some grave news for you guys," Buford said suddenly. "A grave full of **SKELETON AND CEMETERY JOKES!**"

WHY ARE THERE FENCES AROUND CEMETERIES?

Everyone's dying to get in!

WHAT IS A SKELETON'S FAVORITE FOOD?

Spareribs!

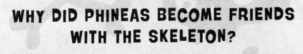

WHY DID PHINEAS BECOME FRIENDS WITH THE SKELETON?

Because he knew it would always lend him a hand.

WHY DIDN'T BALJEET WANT TO SPEND THE NIGHT IN THE CEMETERY?

It was cold! Duh!

A few minutes later, it was Isabella's turn to tell a story.

"There once was a girl who lived next door to an old, spooky Victorian house. One day she noticed a handsome boy sitting on the porch and introduced herself. The boy was wonderful, and so handy and creative that she quickly fell in love with him. But when she went to give him a hug, her hands went right through him!"

"Oh, I don't like this story anymore," Baljeet said, covering his ears. "Tell me when it's over!"

Isabella continued. "The boy told her he had died in a tragic submarine accident hundreds of years ago. And now he was forced to roam the Earth as a spirit! The worst part of it, he told her, was that he could never feel love. The girl stayed in love with him for the rest of her life, even though he could never return her affection."

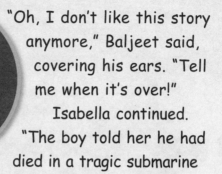

"Cool story," Phineas said. "But would a girl *really* do that? Love a boy that won't love her back?"

"You have no idea." Isabella sighed.

"That tale of unrequited love has bummed me out," said Baljeet.

"Well, I know what will cheer you up," Phineas said. "More jokes! Like some spooky GHOST JOKES!"

WHAT DID THE GHOST SAY TO THE WALL?

Don't mind me, I'm just passing through!

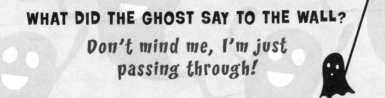

WHAT DID ISABELLA SAY TO THE GHOST?

Whatcha *BOO*-in'?

WHY AREN'T GHOSTS GOOD AT OPERATING HEAVY MACHINERY?

Because they're dead!

WHY DID THE GHOST LIKE TO HANG OUT AT THE CAFÉ?

It was one of his favorite haunts!

A little while later, Baljeet heard a noise in the woods.

"What's that?" he asked, spinning around as a huge, shadowy figure came up behind him. "Is that Bigfoot?"

But it was only Buford with more wood for the campfire. Baljeet was relieved, but pretty scared.

"Can someone please tell some **BIGFOOT JOKES** to lighten the mood?" he asked politely.

WHAT IS BIGFOOT'S BIGGEST EXPENSE?

Shoes!

WHAT'S BIGFOOT'S FAVORITE CANADIAN PROVINCE?

Sasquatchawan.

The gang was having a great time telling spooky stories and jokes. Once again, Phineas had come up with a great idea!

"Hey, you know what being outside under this sky full of stars makes me think of? Zombies!" exclaimed Buford, scaring Baljeet with a bottle of ketchup. "How about some **ZOMBIE JOKES!**"

"Yes, please!" Baljeet cried.

ZOMBIE JOE:

You know that guy Fred? I hate his guts.

ZOMBIE JILL:

So just eat the rest of him!

WHY DOES THE FEMALE GOBLIN LIKE TO PARTY?

She's Goblin-dana and she wants to have fun!

WHAT DID ISABELLA SAY TO THE ZOMBIE?

Who ya chewin'?

DO ZOMBIES EAT POPCORN WITH THEIR FINGERS?

No, they eat the fingers separately!

Soon, it was Ferb's turn to tell a terrifying tale. He held a flashlight up to his face and took a deep breath.

"Kids. Graveyard. Monster. In the bushes. Jumps out." Then he paused dramatically. "Boo!" he shouted, making Phineas and his friends jump back.

"I can't believe that story *scared* you guys," Candace said, annoyed. "There was no vengeful corpse or guy with a hook or anything! You need something *scary*."

"Yeah," Buford said. "Like Frankenstein!"

"You mean Frankenstein's MONSTER," Baljeet corrected. "Frankenstein was the *doctor*."

"Yeah, I know that," Buford said with annoyance. "But I'm scared of doctors!"

"Fine," Candace grumbled. "Does anyone have any **FRANKENSTEIN JOKES?**"

WHY IS FRANKENSTEIN SO FUNNY?

He leaves everyone in stitches!

HOW DID IGOR KNOW WHERE DR. FRANKENSTEIN'S BRAIN WAS?

He had a hunch!

WHY IS A REPAIRED FRANKENSTEIN MONSTER LIKE A FIRESIDE GIRL?

They are both covered with patches!

WHY IS DR. FRANKENSTEIN SO POPULAR?

He's good at making friends.

Candace wasn't impressed with anything she had heard so far. She had a much scarier tale to tell!

"On the corner of Spooky Avenue and Horrible-Head-Chopped-Off Lane, there was an old spooky house. The Johnson house! Not Jeremy Johnson, some other people named Johnson," she explained. "Everyone said the house was haunted and that if you went in, you would never come out!"

Candace continued. "One day, a kid dared his friends to stay overnight in the old, scary, spooky, scary house."

"You know," Buford interrupted, "just because you keep saying 'scary,' it doesn't *make* it scary."

"Just listen!" Candace shouted.

"The kids camped out in the creepy, old living room. All through the night they heard weird groaning noises, the clanking of chains, and eerie screams! It seemed like the terrifying night would never end, but finally, the sun rose. The kids proudly ran outside.

"'Hey, everybody,' the kids called out to people passing on the street. 'We spent the night in the old Johnson house and nothing happened!' But the people walking by just ignored them . . . as if no one could even see them."

Candace paused and looked around, waiting for the shivers of terror she expected. But no one seemed to understand her story.

Candace was annoyed. "No one could see the kids! The people passing by didn't know they were there. They passed right through them like..."

But still no one seemed to follow what she was saying.

"People passed through them because they were *ghosts*! Get it? It's spooky. Oh, forget it!" she shouted.

"I liked your story, Candace," said Isabella. "Haunted house stories are my favorite. Why don't we all tell some **HAUNTED HOUSE JOKES?**"

WHAT TIME IS IT WHEN YOUR HOUSE IS HAUNTED?
Time to get a new house!

 **BALJEET:** Part of me thinks my house is haunted.

 BUFORD: What does the *rest* of you think?

WHY WERE THE GHOSTS UPSET AFTER THEY MOVED INTO THE HOT HAUNTED HOUSE?

They found out it didn't have scare-conditioning!

PHINEAS: Hey, Ferb, what do haunted houses and sea monsters have in common?

FERB: What?

PHINEAS: Absolutely nothing! But it seemed like a good way for me to tell some SEA MONSTER JOKES!

WHERE DOES NOSEY, THE LAKE NOSE MONSTER, SLEEP?

A *water* bed.

WHY DID THE LAKE NOSE MONSTER SWIM ACROSS THE OCEAN?

To get to the other tide.

WHAT DID THE OCEAN SAY TO THE SEA MONSTER?

Nothing, it just waved!

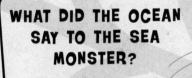

"You know what I think are really scary? Werewolves," Baljeet said. "Let's tell some **WEREWOLF JOKES!**"

WHAT DO WEREWOLVES SAY WHEN THEY GREET EACH OTHER?
Howl ya doin'!

WHAT DID THE WEREWOLF EAT AT THE FANCY RESTAURANT?

The waiters!

KNOCK-KNOCK *Who's there?*

CARL *Carl who?*

CARL THE POLICE, THERE'S A WOLF OUTSIDE!

"Okay, my turn!" Buford suddenly shouted.
"Once there was a kid who was kind of a bully.
In other words, he's the hero of the story.
Anyway, whenever this kid saw a spider, he
would squash it."

"That's not very nice," Baljeet said
squeamishly.

"One night," Buford continued, "this kid
squashed a spider, and then heard a strange

little noise, almost as if the spider was making a last cry for help. Then the kid heard a strange rustling noise in the bushes. The kid was getting scared, so he ran home. The noise got louder," he said. "Even inside the house, he could hear it coming closer!

"The boy ran into his bedroom and closed the door. Then he heard the noise moving toward his room and scratching on his door!"

"The kid couldn't stand it any longer!" Buford yelled. "So he opened the door and standing right there in front of him was a gigantic spider!"

"Oops, I think I left the water running back at home. I had better go check!" Baljeet cried.

Buford grinned evilly. "The kid thinks he's a goner but suddenly realizes, 'Hey, wait a second! You're a bully, just like me. Let's be a team.'

"And from that day on," said Buford, "they lived happily ever after. The end."

"That was *terrible*!" Baljeet complained. "Only a bully would like that ending."

"How about if I give you a mega-wedgie?" Buford challenged.

"Did I mention how much I loved that story?" Baljeet said with a whimper.

Phineas tried to lighten the mood. "Hey, how about some jokes about **SPIDERS AND OTHER CREEPY CRAWLIES?**"

BUFORD: What do Phineas and Ferb have in common with a giant beetle?

BALJEET: I don't know. What?

BUFORD: They both "bug" Candace. Get it? Like, if the beetle was bugging her.

BALJEET: I get it, Buford. Your jokes are only slightly less painful than your wedgies.

PHINEAS: What do you get when giant spiders encircle the planet?

FERB: A world wide web.

WHAT HAS 9 EYES, 15 LEGS, AND SHARP TEETH?

I don't know either, but it's crawling up your leg!

Just then, Perry the Platypus waddled into the backyard.

"Oh, there you are, Perry!" Phineas exclaimed. Then he leaned in closer to his pet and listened carefully. "Perry wants to hear some **JOKES ABOUT OTHER KINDS OF MONSTERS** and more scary things!"

WHAT'S THE ONLY THING A GELATIN MONSTER IS AFRAID OF?
A spoon!

WHO SCARES DR. DOOFENSHMIRTZ MORE THAN PERRY THE PLATYPUS?

Scary the platypus!

WHEN IS THE WORST TIME FOR A BLACK CAT TO CROSS YOUR PATH?

When you're a mouse!

WHY DIDN'T THE HEADLESS HORSEMAN EVER WIN A RACE?

He could never get ahead.

Now it was time for Baljeet to tell his spooky story to his friends.

"Prepare to be borified," Candace grumbled.

"Prepare to be *petrified*," Baljeet said eerily. "But first, I must explain to you about blood types. There are four possible blood types: A, B, AB, and O. There is also the Rh factor, which can be positive or negative. Now for the scary story. Whereas most vampires can drink any type of blood, there was once a very unlucky O-negative vampire who could only drink type O blood with a negative Rh factor. This rare blood type only accounted for seven percent of the population."

Baljeet continued. "So, the hapless vampire roamed the streets, searching for victims. He would give them a blood test, but by the time he figured out their blood type, they had escaped."

"They probably died of boredom," Buford said, yawning.

Baljeet rolled his eyes. "Finally, the hungry vampire found a blood bank filled with O negative. He was as happy as a bat in a cave! He drank and drank to his heart's content, but he lost track of time, and suddenly the sun was rising...."

"Before the vampire could find shelter, the rays of the sun hit him and turned him to dust. He met his untimely end by being vacuumed away by a janitor. The end!"

NICE STORY, BALJEET!

HEMATOLOGY-RELATED STORIES *NEVER* FAIL TO ENTERTAIN.

"Candace once thought SHE was a vampire," Phineas commented.

"Wait," Candace interrupted her brother. "You shrank yourself down to microscopic size. You own a milkshake bar on an asteroid. And you think it's weird that I thought *I* was a vampire?!"

"Fair enough," Phineas agreed. "Then you won't mind if we tell a few **VAMPIRE JOKES!**"

ISABELLA: Why wouldn't the monster kiss the vampire?

PHINEAS: Why?

ISABELLA: He had *bat* breath!

WHAT IS DRACULA'S FAVORITE SPORT?
Batminton!

WHERE DO THEY PUT VAMPIRE CRIMINALS?
In *blood* cells!

HOW DO VAMPIRES CROSS THE SEA?
Blood vessels!

"Great jokes and stories everybody," Phineas said. "But it's getting late. We'd better head inside."

Candace was outraged. "That's *it*? Those are your scary stories? This is the least scary night of my *life*!"

"Hiiiii, Candace," came a voice from the darkness. She whirled around to see a figure emerge from the shadows. It was Jeremy Johnson's little sister, Suzy! Nothing scared Candace more than her!

"**Ahhhhhhhhh!**" Candace screamed.

"Well, what do you know?" Phineas said with a shrug. "Guess Candace had a scary night after all!"